# BORKA

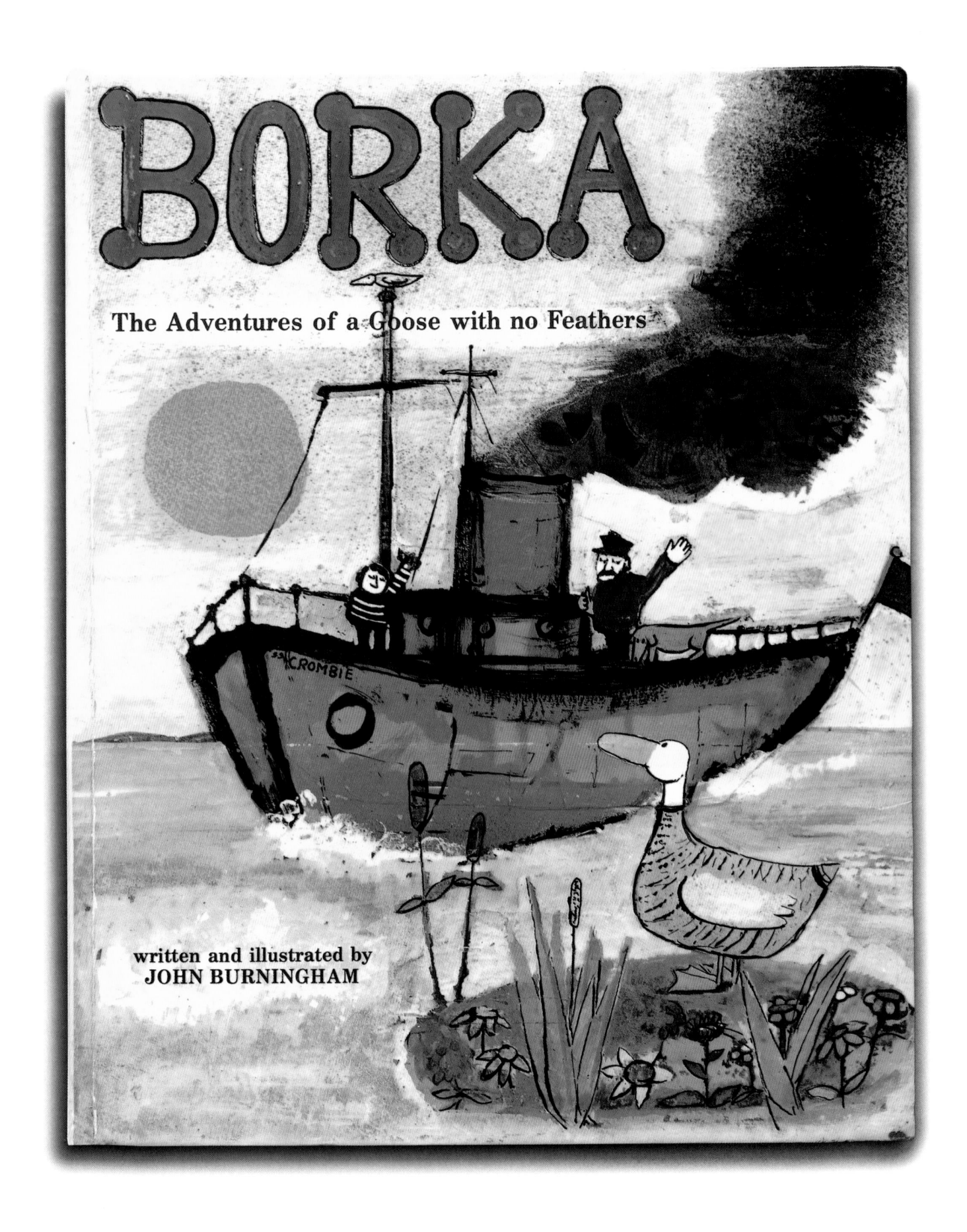

*Cover from the first edition of* Borka, *published in 1963.*

THIS story began a long time ago. I was in my late twenties and had recently joined Jonathan Cape as Literary Director. One of our manuscript readers told me that a friend of hers, who happened to live a few hundred yards from my office in Bedford Square, had recently completed a picture book for children. He had carried the book around London but with no success. I rang the artist to arrange a meeting. I went round to his basement flat in Percy Street and he showed me his book. It was called *Borka, The Adventures of a Goose with no Feathers*. I was greatly impressed and, even more importantly, I was moved by the book. There was one picture especially which I found extraordinary. It was of a mother goose knitting a vest for its child born with no feathers and the child looks on poised and eagerly expectant. The artist was John Burningham. I expressed my admiration but I also explained that I had never published a children's book and, beyond that, Jonathan Cape had never published even a single picture book. Our fame, which was considerable, rested upon innovation in the adult field, both fiction and non-fiction.

I offered to champion *Borka* and to show it to our Chairman, George Wren Howard (co-founder of the company). I said that I would have to take the portfolio of artwork to my office. With some reluctance John entrusted it to me and off I went. Now, Wren Howard liked the book though I can't say he loved it. Patiently he explained to me that to publish a book in colour it was necessary to share costs by arranging for the book to be published in several languages. This, he said, would not be easy to achieve with an unknown artist. For a week or so I looked at the illustrations every day and they grew and grew on me.

Then I went back to Wren Howard and said please could we just go ahead regardless. I promised not to make a habit of this kind of request. He said, 'Okay'.

The rest is history. *Borka* was bought for translation by no fewer than eight foreign publishers and also by Random House in America. We also reprinted our own edition several times. The final accolade came when *Borka* won the Kate Greenaway Award as the best picture book of the year. This had never before been given to a first book. Wren Howard was so impressed that he suggested I might look for another artist. And that is how we came to publish Quentin Blake.

This new edition celebrates the fortieth anniversary of *Borka*. During the intervening years, John has produced some forty books. The variety is extraordinary. *Borka* was followed by a book that comes close to perfection, *Mr Gumpy's Outing*. At this point John began to explore a variety of themes, and of these my favourite is *Granpa*. I have boundless and ever-increasing admiration for his work. He is, to my mind, quite simply the greatest British illustrator for children. The aspect of his talent that I admire above all is his capacity to move readers - children and adults equally.

TOM MASCHLER

John Burningham

# BORKA

## The Adventures of a Goose with no Feathers

JONATHAN CAPE
London

# For Helen

BORKA
A JONATHAN CAPE BOOK 0 224 06494 0

Published in Great Britain by Jonathan Cape,
an imprint of Random House Children's Books

Jonathan Cape edition published 1963
This edition published 2003

1 3 5 7 9 10 8 6 4 2

Copyright © John Burningham, 1963

The right of John Burningham to be identified as the author of this work has been
asserted in accordance with the Copyright, Designs and Patents Act 1988.

RANDOM HOUSE CHILDREN'S BOOKS
61–63 Uxbridge Road, London W5 5SA
A division of The Random House Group Ltd
RANDOM HOUSE AUSTRALIA (PTY) LTD
20 Alfred Street, Milsons Point, Sydney,
New South Wales 2061, Australia
RANDOM HOUSE NEW ZEALAND LTD
18 Poland Road, Glenfield, Auckland 10, New Zealand
RANDOM HOUSE (PTY) LTD
Endulini, 5A Jubilee Road, Parktown 2193, South Africa

THE RANDOM HOUSE GROUP Limited Reg. No. 954009

www.**kidsatrandomhouse**.co.uk

A CIP catalogue record for this book is available from the British Library.

Printed and bound in Singapore

Once upon a time there were two geese called Mr and
Mrs Plumpster.

They lived on a deserted piece of marshland near the East Coast of England, where their ancestors had once lived many years before. There they built their nest and laid their eggs.

Each spring the Plumpsters came back to the marshes and mended their nest. Then Mrs Plumpster settled down to lay her eggs, and Mr Plumpster kept guard.

He hissed at anything that came near the nest.
  Sometimes he hissed even if there was nothing in sight.
It made him feel important.

Then the eggs began to hatch.  One fine spring morning there were six baby Plumpsters in the nest.

Mr Plumpster was delighted, and he invited his friends round to celebrate.

The young geese were given names.  They were

Archie

Freda

Jennifer

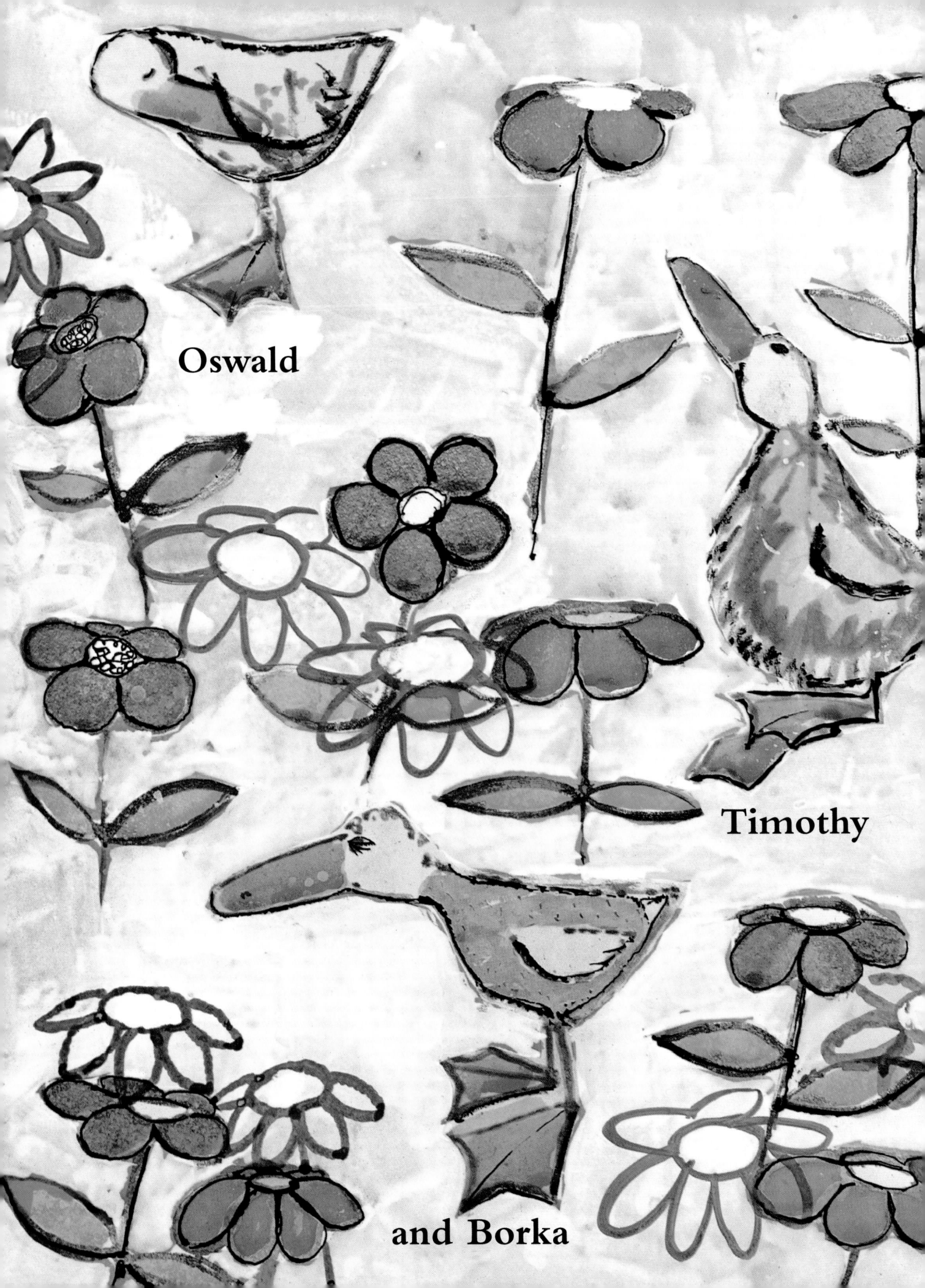

Oswald

Timothy

and Borka

Now all geese look very much alike when they are young, but right from the start there was something odd about Borka. Borka had a beak, wings, and webbed feet like all her brothers and sisters, but she did not have any feathers.

Mr and Mrs Plumpster were very worried about this. They called in the doctor goose who examined Borka carefully. He said there was nothing wrong with her except that she did not have any feathers. "A most unusual case," he went on, and he thought for a long while. Then he told Mrs Plumpster that there was only one thing to do. She must knit some feathers for Borka.

So Mrs Plumpster got out her knitting needles and
set to work. Of course she could not knit real
feathers, but she made a kind of grey woollen jersey
as much like feathers as she could.
  When she had finished, she called Borka
and tried it on her. Borka was delighted,
and flapped around with joy, because
she had always been chilly at night.

She went and showed the other young geese, but they just laughed at her. This made her very unhappy and she went into a patch of tall reeds and cried.

Now by this time the other young geese were learning to fly and to swim properly. But Borka did not like joining in because the others teased her, and so she got very behind with her lessons.

Nobody noticed that she was not attending. Mr and Mrs Plumpster were far too busy. Borka did try to learn to swim, but whenever she went into the water, her jersey took such a long time to dry afterwards that she soon gave up.

By now the summer was almost over. The weather was getting cooler and the geese were becoming restless. At this time of year they always went to a warmer land where it was easier to find food.

The Plumpsters began getting ready to leave. They covered their nest with twigs and rushes to keep it safe through the stormy winter.

Then one day it became really cold and wet.

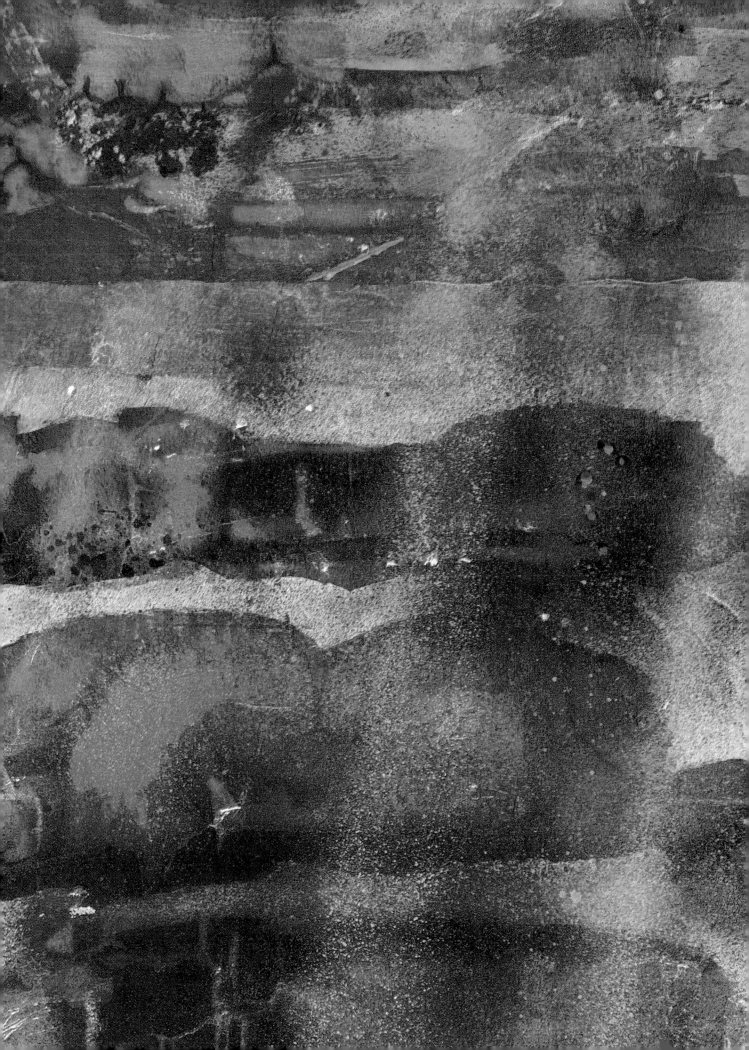

The geese shivered, and knew it was time for them to go. They chose one wise old goose to lead them and they all flew away.

But Borka did not go. She could not fly. Instead she went and hid, and watched them leave. Nobody noticed that she was missing. They were all too busy thinking of the journey ahead. As the geese disappeared into the grey sky, tears trickled down Borka's beak.

She did not know what to do.

It was drizzling, and she wandered off, hoping to find a dry place for the night. It was already getting dark when she came to a line of boats moored in the estuary. Borka chose one that had no lights on board, and she walked up the gangplank.

She was just going down into the hold of the boat when there was a loud bark. A dog came rushing out, which gave Borka a terrible fright. But the dog, seeing it was only a goose, stopped barking and introduced himself. He was called Fowler.

Borka explained that she only wanted to stay under cover for the night, so Fowler showed her into a part of the hold where there were some old sacks for her to lie on. She was so tired that she fell asleep almost at once.

Now the boat, which was called the *Crombie*, belonged to Captain McAllister. Late that night he and his mate, whose name was Fred, came back, and they decided to sail early in the morning before it was light. Fowler forgot all about Borka, who was still asleep in the hold.

It was not until they were well on their way that he
remembered, and told the Captain.

"Well, well!" said Captain McAllister.

"A goose on board! She'll have to work her passage if
she's coming with us to London."

Borka was soon very
friendly with the
Captain, Fred and, of
course, with Fowler.
She coiled pieces of
rope with her beak,
picked up crumbs
from the floor and
helped in any
way she could.
    In return she
was given
plenty of
good food.

At last the *Crombie* steamed into the Thames and they
were nearing London. Captain McAllister began to
wonder what to do with Borka when they got there.
 He decided to leave her in Kew Gardens, which is a
large park where lots of geese live all the year round.

When they came to the place where the river flows past Kew Gardens, Captain McAllister lifted Borka over the railings and put her with the other geese. She was sorry to say goodbye to her friends but they promised to come and visit her on their next trip to London.

The geese at Kew did not mind that Borka had no feathers. There were already so many strange kinds of birds in the gardens. Nobody laughed at her grey woollen jersey and all the geese were very friendly, especially one called Ferdinand. Ferdinand cared for Borka and taught her to swim really well. She is still living there happily and whenever Captain McAllister and Fred and Fowler come to London they call in to see her.

So if you are in Kew Gardens at any time and you see a goose who looks somehow different from the others – it might well be Borka.

ABOUT 40 years ago, most of my time was spent doing posters for London Transport. I had had the idea for a book about a goose with no feathers for at least two years. I decided to call the goose Borka. As far as I can remember, Borka was the name of a tame goose in the Moscow zoo or circus.

As a child and pupil at Summerhill School, and later as an art student, I had spent much time around the estuaries of East Anglia, which became the background influence for the *Borka* pictures.

A friend of mine called Ann Carter, who was a translator and reader for the publisher Jonathan Cape, persuaded me to make a rough dummy and layout of the book. She said she would get Tom Maschler at Jonathan Cape to have a look at it.

The book was published and from then on I was set on course for writing and illustrating children's books.

I am amazed to find that so much time has passed since the book was published, and I am honoured that all these years on, the first book I created for children is still being enjoyed by them all over the world.

JOHN BURNINGHAM

*Rough drawings in preparation for the 1963 edition of* Borka.
*This page, Captain McAllister lifts Borka over the railings in Kew Gardens.*

*Borka bids farewell to her friends aboard the* Crombie.

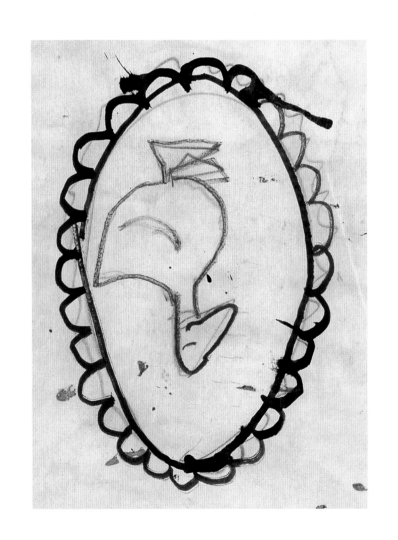